I0538667

Living Separate Lives

Four Friends, One Secret
and The Weekend That Changed Their Destiny

A CHRISTIAN NOVELLA

Paulette Harper

Thy Word Publishing

© 2013 Paulette Harper

All rights reserved. No part of this book may be used or reproduced, stored in or introduced into a retrieval system, or transmitted in any form or by any means without the express written consent of the Publisher of this book.

Living Separate Lives is a work of fiction. Names, characters, places, and incidents either are the product of the author's imagination or are used fictitiously. Any resemblance to actual persons living or dead, events, or locales is entirely coincidental.

Published by Thy Word Publishing

Editor: Felecia S. Killings of PFL Publishing:
www.liyahamore.weebly.com

Cover Design and Images: Tyora Moody / Tywebbin.com

Interior Design and Typesetting: Glenda Wallace/
www.interiorbookdesigns.com

Author Website: www.pauletteharper.com

Amazon Author Profile and Full Book List:
http://tinyurl.com/mvzj65j

Library of Congress Cataloging-1-979115361

ISBN-10: 098996910X
ISBN-13: 978-0-9899691-0-9

Published and printed in the United States of America

Acknowledgments

Jeremiah 29:11
Contemporary English Version (CEV)
I will bless you with a future filled with hope — a
future of success, not of suffering.

I give thanks to God for once again allowing me the privilege to pen yet another book. Without Him none of this would be possible. He continues to amaze me. I praise Him because He gives me what to write and the stories to tell and for that I am eternally grateful. My desire is to bring Him glory with each book I write.

I'm thankful for my family and friends who continue to support me by their prayers, contributions and encouragement.

A special shout out to my daughters Felecia and Ariel for blessing me with two beautiful granddaughters who call me their "MiMi."

Much love to Mike Lopez for giving me a place to write my novels when I come back home.

Special thanks to the book clubs that have supported me by reading my books and those who will. You have many books to pick from. Thank you for adding mine to your selection.

I pray that something you read in the pages of this book will draw you closer to our Heavenly Father.

I introduce you to *Living Separate Lives*.

Chapter 1

"Who cares anyway if I die? I hate my life; I curse the day I was born," said Candace as she rolled out of her twin bed to face yet another day of sheer disappointments. Her feet landed on the beige, shaggy, dirty carpet that had seen better days. As she sat on the edge of her bed, she looked around the small apartment as though she was expecting to see something different, but nothing had changed.

"Lord, can I get a break? Can something good happen in my life?" she cried as her head collapsed in her hands. She knew within herself that today would be like all the rest: gloomy, sad, and most of all, lonely. After all she had experienced in life, how could she think today would be any different?

Candace lived in a small studio apartment off of School Street in the city of Pittsburg, California, a city surrounded by the beautiful San Francisco Bay Area. Her apartment had enough room for only one dresser and a nightstand, which she got at the neighborhood Goodwill store.

The walls of her apartment were dirty from years of cigarette smoke that didn't escape out of the window. Her kitchen table was made of plywood, which she covered with a red tablecloth. The table was encompassed by two chairs, one for her and the other one she had hoped would be occupied by someone who genuinely wanted to be with her. The blue and cream décor in her kitchen came from visiting the neighborhood garage sales. Her neighbors knew her so well because of the frequent visits she made to their sales. Although Candace always had a roof over her head, she did not like the environment in which she lived. After looking intently at her dwelling place, she lay back on her bed and stared at the ceiling. Her thoughts shifted from her disappointing apartment to her anger about the issues she had to deal with, problems that had been with her for years, issues with her family.

Since high school, life was hard for Candace. Almost every decision she made never retuned a good dividend. The men in her life came and went, except for Derrick. He stayed the longest, but his bout with kidney failure ended whatever dreams she had of getting out of what she called the "ghetto." Derrick was her sure ticket to a better life, she'd hoped. The only consolation to his memory was the pictures on the stained walls and a locket she wore around her neck.

Candace grew up with both parents and two siblings. Her sister, Monique, was three years younger than her; her brother, Zach, was two years younger. Candace always felt that she got the worse end of the stick when it came to Monique. Monique was light-skinned with long, black, wavy hair, which belonged to her, by the way. Candace's skin tone was a few shades darker than Monique's. She was short in stature, five feet, three inches tall, to be exact. She wore her hair down and straight, although it mostly contained black hair extensions, which she bought from the neighborhood beauty supply store.

Monique was the image of her mother, minus a few inches of hair. She stood five feet, eleven inches with a small frame; she could have been chosen as America's Next Top Model. But Monique decided to study law, passing the bar on her first attempt; she then started her own practice and moved it to Los Angeles. Monique and her parents could not figure out why Candace didn't make more of herself. To them, Candace was merely existing and taking up space. They wrote Candace off years ago.

Her parents would say they didn't show favoritism to any of their children, but let Candace tell the story; she would disagree. Candace didn't have a great relationship with her parents, nor did she have one with her sister. She longed to connect with her mother, Vivian, even dreaming of having meaningful conversations with her, but that never materialized. Vivian grew up without love, so showing love was not something she did or knew how to do.

Nothing Candace did was ever good enough for her parents. She realized long ago that they would never validate or accept her for who she was. And that always bothered her. The only relative that Candace found solace in was her baby brother.

Zach was the comic relief in the family and the only one who tried to keep Candace from running away from home when they were teenagers. Despite what he saw from his family, he found laughter to be a source of comfort. A joke at the right time would always make Candace laugh instead of cry many days. Now that he was older, his life revolved around school, his baby, and opening up his own barber shop.

Zach had similar features like his dad. He had a body like LL Cool J's, muscular in build, which required him to spend more time in the gym and less time getting into trouble. His skin tone was the same as Candace's, and his hair was black and curly, which he kept cut low.

Their dad, Robert, didn't care about too much except a good home-cooked meal and the wrestling matches that he saw nightly. He was content to spend his time sitting in his brown leather recliner with a blanket next to the wooden table that had enough room to hold his can of Pepsi, the remote control, and the cordless phone.

While reminiscing about one's family may bring happiness to others, memories of her family only angered Candace even more. The longer she lay there, the angrier she got. In order to avoid another day filled with anger, she started thinking about how much her life would change for the better if only she could win the lotto or meet a rich man. But that wasn't going to happen any time soon, especially if she continued to linger in the bed all day like she had been doing for the last few days. Candace sighed and finally decided to climb out of bed. Maybe today would be her lucky day.

Candace made her way to the small kitchen and began fixing breakfast. Today's meal consisted of a slice of toast and coffee. Once she finished her breakfast, she stepped into the shower and let the warm water soothe her. She grabbed a pair of jeans and a tee shirt, and headed out the door.

Outside her apartment she could hear the normal chanting from the neighborhood kids. "There she goes," the kids began to yell. Candace was often referred to as "crazy Candi" because many times while walking to the corner store to pick up her soda, cigarettes, and a lottery ticket, they often observed her muttering to herself. Whenever they mocked her, she would turn around and yell back at them. "I ain't crazy," she would yell. "I know y'all think I am, but I'm not. I'm talking to God. That's something y'all young hoodlums should think about doing sometimes."

While walking along the street, Candace decided to do something differently. Instead of passing by the church on the way to the store, she decided to go in and pray. She made herself comfortable in one of the pews. The soft music that played inside the church made her thoughts wander to the first time she went to church.

Candace was introduced to Christ by one of her friends, Kaylan. To Candace, going to church was the last thing on her mind or on her agenda. But she figured church couldn't be any worse than being home with people who didn't give love or show love. "I'll give church a try," she said to herself. "Maybe I can find some answers to my probing questions as to why God didn't give me a loving family and why nothing good has happened to me. Maybe the church folks would love me and help me, but most importantly, pray for me," she said to herself.

She remembered the first time she walked into New Life Christian Center on Christmas day. All the people were raising their hands, which was so foreign to her. It didn't seem real. She was feeling something, but didn't know exactly what to call "it" or if "it" had a name. This was one feeling she couldn't identify.

The church décor was beautiful with poinsettias placed around the stage area. For the first time in Candace's life, she thought that maybe this was exactly the thing she needed. When she and Kaylan entered the sanctuary, the usher wanted to sit them close to the front of the church, but Candace would not have it. She leaned toward Kaylan and said, "Oh no, can't we sit near the back? I might need to go to the restroom." Kaylan agreed. Seating them in the front was not a good idea for more reasons than one. And Kaylan didn't want Candace's first visit to New Life to be her last.

Kaylan motioned to the usher, "We'd like to sit in the back, if that's okay." With reservations, the usher directed them to the empty seats in the back of the church. During service, the choir sang songs that Candace had never heard before. Luckily, the words were plastered on the screen for people like her, the unchurched. Yet the sound that came from the choir calmed her apprehension. The choir leader invited everyone to stand and join along. Kaylan turned to Candace, as she stood up to join in on the praise.

"Come on, Candace; it's okay. Let go and let God." Candace looked skeptical.

"Let go and let God," Candace muttered. "What in the world does that mean?" *Maybe Kaylan will educate me on the church lingo later,* she thought. Candace slowly stood on her feet and joined Kaylan and all the church folks who didn't have the same problem as her. Not feeling as comfortable as Kaylan, Candace left her arms by her side.

As the music continued, people began clapping, shouting, and running around the church. Candace's brown eyes widened as big as saucers as she watched all this, and her focus went from the choir to the little lady doing what appeared to be some type of praise dance. All

Candace could do was laugh. A nudge from Kaylan on her arm got her attention back on the choir. About thirty minutes into the singing, the pastor emerged and took the podium. "That's Pastor Jonathan Williams," Kaylan proudly announced to Candace. "That's my pastor," she said with excitement.

"Good morning, saints. This is the day the Lord has made; let us be glad and rejoice," Pastor Williams said in a baritone voice.

"Praise the Lord," echoed the congregation to the pastor; well, everyone except for Candace.

"First, the usher wanted to seat us in the front of the church. Then they wanted us to stand. Now we get to yell back to the pastor?" Candace whispered right before Kaylan let out a loud "Glory to God!" More claps and more shouting came, and the applause became louder. The roar reminded Candace of a sports game when the winning team finally scored. She remembered that, but had no idea "church" was anything like that.

"Today's text comes from John 3:16. You may be seated," said Pastor Williams.

Candace and Kaylan exchanged glances, and Candace's voice let out a soft "Praise the Lord." They immediately started smiling and took their seats.

Candace's five-inch, black stilettos were not the ideal pair of shoes to wear to church. They were cute, but being cute was not good enough. Candace didn't realize that it took preparation to come to church, something she'd have to really consider next time.

Kaylan reached down into her purse that was located on the floor and pulled out her notebook, a Bible, and a pen— all of which Candace had none.

"You taking notes?" Candace inquired. "You didn't tell me to bring a notebook."

"Don't worry. Here you go." Kaylan quietly tore out several pieces of paper from her notebook and handed them to Candace along with a pen.

"The words will be up on the screen, or we can share my Bible," Kaylan said as they moved closer together on the seat. In his message, Pastor Williams talked about the reason why Jesus came to the world and why people needed to be saved; in his message, he explained the real meaning of love. While the pastor was speaking, the ushers were walking around the sanctuary, offering Kleenex to those who were apparently shedding tears. Candace declined the offer. Instead, she wiped the tear from her face with the back of her hand when the pastor began to talk about love, something she yearned for from her family and men.

"God is love, and God showed His love by giving the ultimate sacrifice by sending His son, Jesus," said the pastor. At one point in his message, he stated, "We try to find love in all the wrong places; the void in our lives can only be filled by God's love."

During his message, Candace's mind traveled back to all the times she wanted to be loved by her family, excluding Zach because he did love her. Her mind wondered about the men who had been in and out of her life. The pastor was right; she had been looking for love in all the wrong places. Unable to stop the flow of tears, she realized the reasons why her life was in such chaos.

Loud shouts of "Amen!" startled her, and brought her back from her reverie. At the end of the message, Pastor Williams gave what Kaylan called "an invitation to salvation." Before Kaylan could ask Candace if she wanted to accept Christ, Candace was already making her way down to the altar.

Yes, it truly had been a while since Candace first felt that love and acceptance from others. After the death of Derrick, it was hard for her to see that God really loved her. But as she walked into the church that dreadful afternoon, she decided that it was finally time to make a change.

Chapter 2

Although people envied her for having a perfect life, Kaylan never let money interfere with how she treated people. She lacked for nothing. Her parents were wealthy, very wealthy. They owned several wineries in the Napa County, properties in the Oakland Hills, and several businesses in other states. Her parents lived "The American Dream" and they wanted their children to do the same. Kaylan and her siblings all went to college and graduated summa cum laude. She graduated with her Master's Degree in Business Management. Their mother, Nina, migrated to America from the Philippines; their father, David, was American of African descent. Kaylan had long, brown hair that graced her emerald eyes. She stood five feet, seven inches tall with a small frame. Her smile lit up any room she entered, and her skin was a butterscotch tone.

Kaylan's gorgeous home was located in the Napa region, which was a graduation gift from her parents. It consisted of five bedrooms, three bathrooms, and a three-car garage. Together, she and Bryan, who was Caucasian, had one child, Aisha, who was twelve years old.

Their huge kitchen and great room, with its vaulted ceiling, was perfect for casual entertaining; the formal living room and formal dining room were the ticket for a bit of sophistication. The master suite featured two, huge walk-in closets, one of which was the perfect size for an office. The beautifully landscaped grounds surrounded the pillar-accented porch. Truly, she was blessed.

As Kaylan reflected on her many blessings from God, a phone call interrupted her musing.

"Who could be calling me this early?" Kaylan whispered as she looked at the wall clock, which read 7:00 a.m. She rolled over from her bed, grabbed her cell phone from her nightstand, and answered; however, she didn't recognize the number. Not wanting to disturb Bryan, she got out of bed and headed towards the black recliner in the seating area of their bedroom. Before curling up in the chair, she turned on the table lamp to give the room more light.

"Hello, can I speak with Kaylan?" A voice from the opposite end spoke.

"This is Kaylan. Who am I speaking with?"

"I know it's been a long time, but this is Candace." A few seconds passed before Kaylan spoke.

"Candace Walker, is that you?" Kaylan asked with excitement. Kaylan repositioned herself on the chair.

Candace nodded as if Kaylan could see her. "Yes, it is."

"Oh, my gosh. How have you been? It's been so long."

Candace chuckled. "Yes, I know. I'm doing okay," she said cautiously.

"It's so good to hear from you. Where are you?" Kaylan waited with anticipation for an answer.

"I'm back in Pittsburg. Didn't think I'd return to my old roots, but here I am," replied Candace.

"Well, I'm in Napa County, which isn't far. We have to get together. I'd love to see you," Kaylan retorted.

"Yeah, I think it's time. Do you keep in contact with Tiffany and Jordan?" asked Candace.

"Not like we should. Our schedules are so hectic. But that's no excuse. We've got to do better about staying connected. We should plan something so we can all get together. A little mini-reunion would be so much fun," Kaylan replied.

There was a long silence before Candace spoke. "Well, that would be great." Kaylan detected the uneasiness in Candace's voice. Her curiosity wanted to know why Candace had called after all this time. She cleared her throat before asking.

"Candace, what's going on? I'm picking up that all is not well." Kaylan was persistent, and she was not letting Candace hang up the phone without telling her why she called. Kaylan asked again, "Candace, what's wrong?"

Candace waited a few minutes before replying. "Yeah, there has been a lot going on; not sure where to begin." She paused before continuing. "First, my boyfriend, Derrick, died from kidney failure about three months ago, and I've had a hard time dealing with the loss. I've had plenty of time to think about how my life was in so much chaos." Kaylan could hear Candace's voice begin to quiver as she continued. "I've gotten so far away from God and don't know how to get back on track. What's worse is I just got a layoff notice from my job." Candace cleared her throat and said, "When it rains, it pours."

Kaylan eyes filled with tears while she listened to Candace share her story. She waited before she spoke. "Wow! Candace, I'm so sorry to hear about Derrick. Sounds like you have been through the wringer with one thing after another." Kaylan shook her head. "My heart goes out to you. Candace, what can I do to help you?"

"I'd love to see you sometime next week, if that's possible. Can we meet for coffee and we can talk more then?" Candace asked.

"Yes, Candace, we can," Kaylan replied. "You name the place and I'll take the drive to see you. Whatever you need, we'll work together to get you through this season in your life."

"Okay. I'm looking forward to seeing you next week," Candace said with excitement. "I'll talk to you soon."

After hanging up the phone, Kaylan's heart went out towards Candace. She remembered when Candace refused to take her help years ago when she tried to get her to speak in depth about her life. Things must have gotten pretty bad for Candace to call Kaylan after all this time.

Kaylan's thoughts were racing after the conversation. She set her cell phone on the small table, grabbed some Kleenex located next to the chair, and began to sob and pray.

"Lord, my heart is heavy about Candace. What can I do to help her and bring all of us together?

Fifteen minutes later, the sobs subsided and she reached for her cell phone to see the time. It was 7:30 am. She had two hours to get ready for work. *I must look a mess,* she imagined, with tears running down her face. She grabbed more tissue and cleaned herself up. Minutes later, she rose from the seat, and headed toward the bathroom.

On her way there, she took a look in her closet to decide what she would wear today. She leaned her body up against the door frame, and observed just how blessed she was. Her walk-in closet was big enough to be a bedroom, filled with name brand clothes, some with the price tags still attached. Kaylan, if she wanted to, could change clothes three or four times in a day. Her shoes, too many to count, had a section by themselves, all organized by color.

Kaylan stepped into her closet, grabbed her robe, and headed to her bathroom to take a shower. The warm, running water calmed her nerves, which were rattled a little by the shock of hearing from Candace after all these years. Her mind wondered if she had done enough to help Candace. Had she done enough to help the less fortunate? Could she have done more?

Kaylan's heart ached for people who were less fortunate and those who didn't grow up in a loving family environment. Maybe that's why she was drawn to Candace. She recalled the many times she tried to extend her generosity to Candace by offering her help. But Candace's pride kept her from accepting any, as she called it, "handouts". Kaylan just couldn't understand why her friend continued to live the way she did, knowing that at the drop of a hat, Kaylan would have done anything for her. All that mattered now was how she was going to help Candace get her life together.

She made her way out of the bathroom and had just enough time to eat breakfast. The smell of bacon was lingering in the air, which caused her to be hungry. She strolled into her kitchen and found the pot of coffee already made and her breakfast prepared by Bryan. He posted a note on the microwave that read, "I love you. See you tonight."

She poured herself some coffee, retrieved her plate out of the microwave, and pulled out a chair at the wooden table so she could eat her meal. Kaylan stared at the note Bryan left for her, and his thoughtfulness brought back memories of how they met.

During college, Kaylan prayed that God would give her a mate. Not just any mate, but someone who was progressive, someone who wanted the finer things in life, and someone that, most importantly, loved Jesus and had a heart for the less fortunate. She believed God answered her prayer when she met Bryan during her freshman year.

One day while she walked down the hall, tightly holding her books with her eyes focused on her schedule, she did not notice Bryan walking directly towards her. Without breaking his stride, he accidentally bumped into her. She lost her balance, and all of her books scattered across the floor. As Bryan assisted her with her belongings, their eyes gazed at one another. She was the most beautiful woman Bryan had ever seen.

When they started dating, Bryan shared with Kaylan that his parents wanted him to marry someone of his color. But Bryan was determined not to let his parents dictate who he was going to love. He tried to assure Kaylan that his family would look beyond her color and see her for the beautiful woman she was. Kaylan could never understand how people who said they were Christians refused to accept someone based on the color of their skin. Thinking about these memories caused tears to fill her eyes, and she was immediately brought back to the present.

Kaylan finished her breakfast and tidied up the kitchen; she headed for the bedroom where she would do one final inspection. She decided on the black wrap dress that highlighted her curves and the four-inch black red bottom pumps that Bryan purchased for her. She put the finishing touches on her makeup by applying some Bobby Brown Blackberry lipstick. A light blot of powder was reapplied to remove the shine from her forehead and cheeks. Satisfied with her appearance, she grabbed her purse, keys, and briefcase and headed out the door.

In the garage, Kaylan sat behind the wheel of her Mercedes, pondering on how she could get the ladies together for a "mini-retreat". She admitted that it had been too long since they got together. The business of life should never keep friends apart. She wondered how Jordan and Tiffany were doing. She knew each of the ladies had their own personal demons to deal with and their own issues that impacted each one differently. She thought about Jordan with the challenges she faced being unequally yoked with her husband and Tiffany's concern that she would never get married. Clearly, each one of them had gone through some rough challenges in life, but which one, if any, had really been healed? Thinking about her friends caused her to reminisce on the time they all first met.

She met these ladies in her freshman year of high school. There was an immediate bond with them all. They went to the movies, school games, parties, and dinners together. They truly had a sisterhood.

Maybe the retreat could be the start of rekindling their relationship with one another. She knew God had blessed her to be a blessing to others. So she decided to speak with Bryan to get the okay for her to plan a weekend retreat right there on the vineyard. She'd have them all come to her house.

With a plan in mind, Kaylan started up her car and headed to work.

Chapter 3

I'm getting rid of you before you get rid of me, were the thoughts Tiffany rehearsed in her mind as she drove to the Lake Chalet restaurant on Lakeside Drive. She was going to meet Jeffrey, her "boo" there to discuss the nature of their relationship. Lake Chalet was the first restaurant that she and Jeffrey ate at when they first met. Now, ironically, this would be the same place that she would call off their relationship.

Experience had been a great teacher for Tiffany Thomas. At the rate she and Jeffrey were going, it was only a matter of time before he got up the nerve to break her heart like so many of her other boyfriends had done, at least this is what she thought. She heard the same song over and over again; the men she dated all seemed to share the same brain. The rhetoric was exactly alike: "I'm not thinking about getting married, at least no time soon." they would say. They usually made mention of this whenever Tiffany tried to get them to "define their relationship". But that would end right here.

She promised herself that this time she was not going to get dumped first. If anyone was going to do the dumping, it was going to be her. Consequently, she realized that being committed to this relationship was not something that Jeffrey wanted. And Tiffany was ready to cut the cord before it came back to hang her in the end.

Tiffany and Jeffrey arrived at the restaurant at the same time. When she maneuvered her Lexus into the first open stall she could find, she turned her car off and took one last look in the mirror to make sure everything was in place. She closed her eyes, sat in silence for a moment, and said a little prayer: "Lord, I need your strength tonight to help me get through this evening. Give me the exact words to speak. Thank you, in Jesus' name." She unbuckled her seat belt, climbed out of her Lexus, and walked toward the restaurant to meet Jeffrey.

A suited gentleman received her with a smile, swung open the door, and escorted her inside where Jeffrey was waiting patiently. He greeted her with a "Hello". Jeffrey stood, towering over Tiffany at six feet, one inch; he had the most gorgeous, almond-color skin tone. His bald head and goatee reminded Tiffany of how much he resembled Morris Chestnut. Tonight, he wore a pair of brown slacks with a white, long-sleeve turtle neck that fitted snug around his muscular arms. He made it a habit to lift weights, which contributed to his slender frame. He wore the cologne that Tiffany bought for him on his birthday, *Allure*, by Chanel. She got a good whiff when he kissed her on the cheek.

Tiffany wondered if she was doing the right thing by breaking off their relationship. *He looks so good*, she thought. *Maybe I'm going too fast.* She began to vacillate between her emotions— knowing she must do the right thing versus giving in to her flesh.

The hostess, who identified herself as Vickie, jarred Tiffany to the present when she said, "Right this way, please." They were escorted to a quiet spot in the corner of the restaurant at the request of Jeffrey. Jeffrey pulled out a chair for her, and then proceeded to sit across from her in the opposite seat. The hostess handed them their dinner menus, shared what the evening specials were, and took their drink order.

The two of them eased into conversation by discussing the menu options and choosing their meals. Tiffany chose grilled chicken with a baked potato, and Jeffrey settled on the evening special, salmon. Ten minutes later, Vickie returned with their drink order and took their dinner selections.

For the next few minutes, they exchanged small talk about their day, what the weather was like, and how well they were doing on their jobs. During the entire exchange, Tiffany's stomach quivered. She took a swig of her non-alcoholic drink to quell her emotions.

Seeing her in distress, Jeffrey cocked his head to one side and asked, "What's wrong with you tonight?"

Tiffany's eyes widened. "Just have a lot on my mind. I have to make some difficult decisions about my future."

Jeffrey took a sip of his drink. "I hope I'm included in that future." Vickie could not have timed it more perfectly as she returned with their piping-hot dishes, just in time for Tiffany to avoid Jeffrey's last remark. Before they ate, they fell silent for a moment of prayer, after which they resumed their subtle conversation and ate their delicious meals.

Tiffany wasted no time in addressing her agenda. "I've been thinking about our conversations of late, about marriage, and the direction of our relationship."

"Okay," Jeffrey said gingerly. "What about it?" he asked between bites.

"You made it perfectly clear that you have no intentions of marrying me anytime soon."

Jeffrey shot back. "That's correct; but that doesn't mean I won't marry you at all. I have strong feelings for you, but I'm not ready to settle down just yet."

She could hear the sternness in his voice. "That's fine, and I respect you for that; but since we are not on the same page with the marriage thing, I believe we need to call off our relationship," responded Tiffany. "I don't want to waste my time holding onto a *maybe* proposal."

Jeffrey's jaw dropped. He thought he was going to be able to string her along for a lot longer than this. "Are you breaking up with me?"

Tiffany nodded in agreement and continued. "Yes. This relationship is not going in the right direction."

Jeffrey leaned back in his chair and said, "Alright." Still having a half glass of his drink remaining, he grabbed it, and finished it off in one big swallow. He placed the empty glass on the table, stood up, and walked out of the restaurant, never to see Tiffany again.

<><><>

Tiffany parked her white Lexus in front of her home, but made no effort to get out. She sat and reflected on the dinner date she just had with her now ex-boyfriend. She unbuckled her seat belt and rolled down the window to allow the evening breeze to hit her face. She continued listening to her Tamela Mann CD and allowed the melody to calm her racing heart.

When the song, "Take Me to the King" came on the stereo, she began to sing along as she leaned her head back on the headrest. At that moment, she could identify with the words of the song. Tiffany was frustrated with dating men—uncommitted men. When she glanced out the window and saw a couple that was approaching her car holding hands and laughing with one another, it caused her heart to ache.

All she needed was Jesus and Jesus alone; at least that's what she said after the last few men dumped her. "I don't need any of those uncommitted brothas," she said silently to herself. "They just can't handle a strong-willed sista like me."

She'd worked her way up to become one of the department managers at East Bay Utility Company in the Bay Area. She had a six-figure income and her own home nestled in the beautiful Piedmont Hills in Oakland, California. The utility company provided a really nice retirement plan. She had all the material things that anyone could have ever wanted; but true, lasting love was something missing in her life. The time clock was ticking, and her chances of ever having a family were slowly decreasing.

Tiffany had recently dated several men, one being Deacon Lewis from New Castle Missionary Baptist

Church. She wanted her relationship with Deacon Lewis to be kept a secret to avoid any gossip in the church; but no, Deacon Lewis let it be known in one of the men's fellowship meetings that they were dating. She was so hurt when she heard that the men told their wives, and they told their friends and before she knew it, she was getting neck rolls and cutting eyes from the women who evidently thought he was sent from God for them.

She decided after that fiasco not to date anyone in her church again. Her actions to call the relationship off (if that's what it was after dating him for only four months) were warranted, as far as she was concerned. It only took her one time to learn a valuable lesson: that men gossip just like, or more than, women. *If he told something as simple as the fact that they were dating, when she told him not to, what else would he tell?* She never flunked a class in school, and she certainly was not going to flunk this one with men, at least not with Deacon Lewis. Once she saw a man for who he really was, that was it! "Farewell, Godspeed, and adios; I'm done with you," she would say.

Tiffany was not one for drama. She avoided it like the plague. To some men, she was considered high maintenance; because of her status, she was a high-class "diva", they would say. But she paid a great price getting to where she was. Working her way up the corporate ladder took commitment and determination. She made plenty of sacrifices and she was finally seeing some results. Taking those evening classes, working long hours, and saying no to the latest shoe sales paid off. She had come too far to settle for just any man.

Tiffany shifted her eyes and turned away from the couple; she looked at the picture of her and Jeffrey hanging on her key ring, which brought back memories of happier times they'd had. During those better moments, Jeffrey would sometimes surprise her during her lunch break with a picnic in the park; she remembered the "I love you" texts that would come every morning at 8:00 a.m.; the many times they took a ride down the coast; and the many massages he gave her after working those long hours.

Tiffany and Jeffrey had dated for only two years, just long enough for the spark to fizzle and the flaws of each other to be revealed. They met on Christianmatchmaker.com, an online social network for singles with six-figure incomes. Against her friend's advice, she went ahead and registered for a six-month membership. "Don't do it," Jordan said. Jordan told Tiffany that some of the men on those social networking sites lie and fabricate the truth, and she wasn't sure if that was the way God intended Christians to meet.

Tiffany recalled the conversation she had with Jordan again. "I know I haven't been saved long," Jordan said, "but I always hear this preached at church: 'He who finds a wife finds a good thing and obtains favor from the Lord.' I believe that's Proverbs 18:22, correct?" Jordan asked with conviction. "Well, I believe the man is supposed to find you, right?" Jordan asked. All Tiffany remembered thinking about after that conversation was how someone who hadn't been saved long could tell someone else what to do. But perhaps Jordan was right.

The more Tiffany thought about it, the more she began remembering how her last few broken relationships ended, which made her wonder if maybe her standards were too high. Maybe she needed to take a few things off her "wish list".

Tiffany did everything she could do to meet men, but to no avail; at her age, she was still single, and that wasn't good. She went out to her share of social events, both at church and work, in hopes of meeting her Boaz. But even that didn't work. She didn't think that asking for certain qualities in a man was asking for too much. Her wish list only consisted of having a saved man—a really saved man (none of that I-got-baptized-when-I-was-five business), one who was employed, owned his own car, had his own home, and was ready to settle down. From all accounts, she thought Jeffrey was "the one" based on his profile; but over time, she realized that this "Mr. Right" was Mr. Wrong.

The song on the car stereo changed, and the new tune jarred Tiffany back to the present. She looked at the clock, and saw the lateness of the hour. She decided to go inside and prepare for tomorrow's church service. She rolled up her window, grabbed her keys out of the ignition, and reached for her purse to place her cell phone inside. She stepped out of her car and trotted up the walkway to her home. The minute she entered, she reached for the light switch next to the door, and walked toward the glass table that was located in the foyer.

As she was about to take her shoes off, her cell phone rang. Jordan's face popped up on the screen.

"Great," Tiffany said, hesitating to answer. "How did I know you were going to call?" Tiffany asked when she finally answered her friend's call.

"You knew I was going to call to see how things went. Give me all the details. Y'all still an item?"

"Calm down, girl." Tiffany continued the conversation on the way to her bedroom. When she entered her room, she flipped on the light switch and plopped herself on her bed. She placed the cell phone on the oak wood night stand next to her bed and placed the call on speakerphone to continue chatting with Jordan. She took off her shoes and sat Indian-style on her bed.

"What are you doing?" Jordan asked.

"I'm making myself comfortable. It's been a long evening." Tiffany exhaled and tried to compose herself. The last thing she needed was to hear Jordan say, "I told you so."

Tiffany quickly said, "Well, Jeffrey and I broke up. Now, go ahead and say I told you so."

"Tiffany, that's the last thing in the world I'd say to you. I hear the pain in your voice. I'm so sorry. What happened?" Jordan asked with sympathy.

"He wasn't ready to commit. After all this time, he decided that he wasn't ready to move forward with the relationship; and as we talked more, I realized that our spiritual values were so far apart."

"Oh, okay," Jordan spoke gingerly. "How are you?"

"I'm okay." She paused and then continued. "I learned that when someone says they are saved, I need them to clarify that. People have many different definitions of the word. Even some saints in the church think they are saved, but they really are not."

A minute passed before Jordan spoke. "Yes, you are correct. You know what the Bible says about being unequally yoked. In Amos 3:3, it reads 'How can two walk together unless they agree.'"

Tiffany stood and walked around her bed to her closet. Once there, she pulled out her sky-blue, two-piece sleeper off its hanger, laid it on the edge of her bed, and reclaimed her position.

"You know what, Jordan? For someone that hasn't been saved long, you sure know how to spit out those scriptures. Yeah, the scriptures just roll off your tongue." They both chuckled.

"I'm sorry, Tiffany. I don't mean to be preaching all the time. But you know all we have is the Word to depend on to get us through the rough times."

"I know. It's cool. I'm the oldest and should be telling you a thing or two." Even though Tiffany knew Jordan meant well, she couldn't help but feel some inner contention over the fact that Jordan constantly threw scriptures in her face. Lately, it seemed as if it was becoming more difficult to talk to Jordan like Tiffany used to without Jordan appearing slightly judgmental in their conversation.

Tiffany remained silent for a few minutes, trying to find a way to admit to Jordan that she was right. "Well, my friend, you were right. Maybe the online social networks are good for some; but for this girl, it doesn't work. I've realized that over the past few years, I have been too consumed with trying to find Mr. Right instead of falling in love with Jesus. I put Jesus on the back burner in my quest to find someone to love. My priorities have been wrong and God has shown me that. And Jordan, don't tell me, I already know—God is a jealous God."

"I truly believe that once you put God first, He'll send you someone when you least expect it." Jordan responded. "Waiting on God can seem hard, but it's not. We just need to focus on what He wants and develop our relationship with Him."

After twenty minutes of sharing more about the Word, Tiffany ended the call. She stood up, grabbed her pajamas, and trotted to the bathroom to take a bath in her soaking tub. Once inside the bathroom, Tiffany pulled off her clothes and ran the water as hot as she could tolerate it; she poured some lavender-scented bubble bath in for some added pleasure. The soothing bath relaxed her body and mind as she thought about what she needed to say to the Lord that night in prayer.

Twenty minutes later, she sauntered to her bedroom and got on her knees to pray out loud. "Dear Lord, please forgive me for putting others before you. I repent. I want to do Your will and fulfill Your purpose in my life. You will be my first love from this moment forward. In Jesus' name, Amen." Getting up from the floor, she pulled back the covers, slid in the bed, and went to sleep.

Chapter 4

"**S**top preaching to me. I don't want to hear it anymore. I've had enough of your self-righteousness." The words continued to cut Jordan's heart, words that she never heard before coming from the mouth of her husband, Eric. "You knew how I was before we got married." His tone deepened with every word.

Standing in front of the sink, Jordan was frozen and motionless in the middle of the kitchen. She held the dish towel in one hand and a plate in the other. She turned and faced Eric, whose eyes were cold and hard. The verbal blows kept coming. Her mouth opened wide, but no words could be formed when he uttered the deadly words, "I want a divorce."

Her eyes followed her husband of fifteen years as he opened the refrigerator door and grabbed another beer from the top shelf. He popped the beer open and took a swig. He turned and walked toward the red-oak kitchen table, pulled out a chair, and plopped himself down. A few seconds later, he reached for a coaster from its holder, placed it in front of him, and put the beer on it. He leaned back in his chair and continued his rant.

The white plate that Jordan held slipped from her grip and landed on the hardwood floor, breaking into pieces. Without thinking, she immediately dropped to her knees and picked up some of the pieces with her bare hands. She began to pray over the situation and asked God for strength to get through it.

Eric's eyes widened, and immediately he jumped to his feet to assist her. The chair he was sitting in fell backwards and hit the wall. With his voice cracking, he said, "Let me do this. You go get the broom and dust pan."

When she looked up at Eric, her eyes were filled with tears. She let out a big sigh before she spoke. "Why are you hollering and talking to me in that tone? Don't you dare talk to me like that." Jordan spoke with confidence and boldness for the first time in years. "And what do you mean you want a divorce?"

He continued staring down at the floor, gathering the fragments. "Jordan, will you get the broom and dust pan?" His once strong voice seemed to weaken. Jordan stood to her feet, still bewildered by what just happened. She couldn't understand how, after being married for fifteen years, he could want to end their marriage. Walking cautiously through the kitchen and towards the laundry room, she tried desperately not to break down. She grabbed the broom and dust pan and prayed that God would prepare her for the storm that was brewing.

When she returned to the kitchen, she stood in the door frame and handed him the broom and dust pan. He faced her, but continued with the cleanup. An awkward silence filled the air before she spoke.

"We need to talk. We promised each other that the word "divorce" would never be mentioned in this house." He hesitated to answer her, which only frustrated Jordan more. A flashback of her past reminded her of the old "Jordan". Before she was saved, her sailor's mouth got her into plenty of trouble. Sassy, confrontational, and bossy all rolled into one. She didn't have any problem telling it like it "tis" or "cutting" a person if the situation called for it. She would fight anyone in a minute.

Jordan, a short, curvy, caramel-skin toned woman in her forties, had only been saved for five years; but her old nature was tugging at her to come out. She had put up with his shortcomings after all these years and believed the Lord for his salvation, but that was soon to change.

The clearing of Eric's throat brought her back to the present. Eric returned to his seat and continued the conversation. "Jordan, I'm sorry for hollering at you. And yes, we need to talk." He waved, motioning for her to join him at the table.

Jordan retrieved a glass from the cabinet, opened up the refrigerator, and poured herself a glass of water. She approached the table and collapsed in the seat across from him. She took a sip of the water and set it on the table. Jordan leaned back in the chair, folded her arms, and looked directly at him. "I'm listening."

He leaned forward and licked his lips. "I want a divorce. Since you got saved, you ain't the same. You are always trying to preach to me."

Jordan stared at Eric. "You want to divorce me because I share the scriptures with you and I've changed?"

"No, you preach to me," Eric interrupted. "All this Jesus stuff is making me uncomfortable and I'm not ready to change."

"There is more to this than what you're saying. That ain't no reason to get out of a marriage. Tell me the truth, Eric." Jordan demanded.

"I'm going to move out this weekend," Eric said in a steady voice. He sat back in his chair and began rocking back and forth.

Jordan changed positions in the chair. "What? Why? Eric, this ain't right." Her voice began to break. "Please, Eric, don't leave me." She began to shake her head in denial. "Eric, where you moving to? After fifteen years you want out? No explanation? We've been married all this time, and all of a sudden you want out?"

"I told you why I was leaving," he said in a stern voice. Eric sat up, grabbed his beer can, and tossed it in the trash. "I'm going out for a minute. I'll be back later." He left Jordan at the table, sitting in bewilderment at what had just happened.

She watched as Eric walked out of their home. She could hear the garage door opening and him starting his car. The sound of the garage door closing indicated that he was gone. Jordan sat at the table and said a prayer to God, asking Him to guide her and show her the truth. She knew within herself that Eric wasn't being completely honest and truthful. There was something not adding up.

Moments later, she broke down. She tried her hardest not to cry, but the flood of tears was too much for her to hold back. She cried for her husband who, for some reason unknown to her, wanted to end their marriage. And she cried for herself because of all the emotions she was feeling— rejection, abandonment, and confusion. She thought about her dream of a lasting marriage that now faced extinction. She just didn't understand what in the world she was going to do next, but she knew God would cause this to work for her good. Now was the time she needed to use the scriptures and her faith to walk her through this terrain.

Her mind began racing; she asked herself question after question. Had she missed something all these years? She was taught to submit to her husband and that's what she believed she did. She thought she did everything right—she honored her husband, gave him as much sex as he wanted (even when she didn't feel like it), cooked, took care of the kids and kept his home clean.

She was unprepared and surprised by Eric's behavior. She couldn't believe that he was not the least bit concerned about her feelings or financial well-being. She realized that she had been living in the same house and sleeping in the same bed with someone who was planning on leaving all along. The thought of that sickened her. This was a curve that she didn't expect; this was the conversation that no one in their right mind would ever want to have. This conversation just rocked her world.

As the sobs lessened, she wiped the tears with the back of her hand. She stood up from the table and walked to the bathroom to clean her face. Ten minutes later, after gathering her composure, she walked out of the bathroom and entered their master bedroom to lie down on their king-size bed. Her rest was interrupted by the sound of a cell phone alert, which indicated that there was a text message coming through on Eric's phone. In his haste to leave, he had inadvertently left his phone in the bedroom.

Eric never leaves his phone, she thought. Something inside her kept tugging at her heart about his phone. *Why am I so compelled to grab the cell phone from the nightstand and read the message?* she pondered. Was God giving her a sign? Could the real reason why Eric wanted to leave her and end their marriage be revealed in that message? "Reading someone else's message is unethical and shows distrust," she said out loud. She lay across the bed, staring at the ceiling and pondering the questions that were nagging at her spirit. *How could I explain that to Eric, my reading his messages? What if it's an innocent message coming from his family or his friends? I will be in a hot mess,* she thought. But she couldn't resist the urge to look. Since Eric wasn't going to tell her the truth, she decided to take matters into her hands and read the message.

She rolled over to his side of the bed and grabbed the phone from off the nightstand. As she looked, the face of the screen read, "Where are you, babe? Can't wait to pick up where we left off. Smooches!" In one swift moment, Jordan's world came crashing down. Her worst fears had come upon her. Her husband had been with another woman, breaking the covenant of marriage that Jordan believed so strongly in. She immediately dropped the phone on the bed and sat silently. Feelings of shock, rage, sadness, and betrayal flooded her heart. And she was helpless to do anything about it. Wanting desperately to talk to someone about this news, she picked up the phone and called her friend. Perhaps it was time for someone to comfort her during her time of trouble.

Chapter 5

A week after their phone conversation, Kaylan and Candace decided to meet at Peet's Coffee. Neither one of them knew how the other was going to look after all these years. Since their conversation, Kaylan had gotten Bryan's "okay" about the girls' weekend retreat that would be held at their home in Napa. Kaylan was excited about seeing her friends and even more excited about planning the event.

Kaylan rolled her black Mercedes into the parking lot and found a spot right in front of the door. She turned off her ignition and unbuckled her seat belt. She sent Candace a text to see if she had arrived.

"I've just pulled up. Right in front. Are you here?"

Seconds later, a reply text came in from Candace. "Yes. I'm inside." Kaylan climbed out of the SUV, grabbed her designer purse, and placed her cell phone inside. She reached for her sweater that was located on the back seat of the car and slid it on. She strolled into the coffeehouse where Candace met her at the door. They greeted one another with a hug that lasted for several minutes.

When they finally released each other, they took a head-to-toe look at one another. Kaylan had decided to wear something casual. She wore a pair of Michael Kors jeans and a black, sleeveless, lace tunic. For her shoes, she'd decided on her black, four-inch stilettoes. She finished it off with her large, gold, hoop earrings and gold necklace.

Candace, on the other hand, wore jeans with a black, long-sleeve shirt that had the words "You Rock" spelled out on it with rhinestones. She wore black flats that appeared to be on their last days. Her hair was in a ponytail. She had a Red Cross body bag that accented her wardrobe. She appeared thinner since the last time they had seen each other. Life had not been good to

Candace, and the evidence was written all over her face. She looked worried and tired.

Once inside Peet's, they walked toward the cashier to place their drink order.

"Candace, how are you?" Kaylan asked. Her joy was palpable. "What would you like to drink? It's on me."

Candace seemed relieved. "Thanks, Kaylan. I appreciate that." They placed their drink order and walked to the waiting station while the barista made the drinks.

"To answer your question," Candace said, "I'm doing okay." She gave Kaylan a pained smile. "I could be doing a whole lot better." Minutes later, their names were called. They picked up their drinks and found an empty table in the front of the establishment next to a window. They slid into their seats and placed their drinks on the table. They made themselves comfortable while easing into their conversation.

"Girl, it's so good to see you," Kaylan told her friend.

Candace gave a dry smile. "Same here. I know you were shocked to hear my voice on the other end of the call." She clasped her hand over her drink.

Kaylan took a sip of her drink. "Yes, but I was quite glad to hear from you. Your phone call made me realize just how long it had been since we talked."

Candace responded slowly. "I know, and for me to call and dump all my junk on you didn't help." She took a sip of her drink.

Kaylan shook her head in disagreement. "Girl, we go back to high school. You didn't dump anything on me that I didn't want to hear. I'm just glad you called." Kaylan sighed. "We need each other."

Candace looked skeptical. "Kaylan, don't anyone need me. People gave up on me long ago." Tears welled up in Candace's eyes. Kaylan reached into her purse, handed her some tissue, and placed the rest of it on the table. Kaylan looked intently at her.

"That's not true. I'm not one of those people who gave up on you. Don't put me in that same boat. Why you feel that way?"

Candace shrugged her shoulders. "All the stuff that has happened in my life, no one even bothered to reach out to me. Y'all living large and I'm living in misery." Candace words cut Kaylan's heart. Clearly, Candace had developed bitterness, and it showed in her speech. A moment passed before Kaylan spoke.

"Wait a minute, Candace. I can only speak for myself. You are right. I should have tried harder to stay connected, but that goes both ways, correct? I don't know what you mean by living large, but everything I have, I've earned with hard work," Kaylan retorted. Kaylan was surprised at herself. She felt Candace's pain, but didn't want her to get away with not owning up to her own decisions in life. She realized that Candace had it hard, but she had the same opportunities presented to her; however, she chose to go in another direction.

Candace's eyes widened. "I know, Kaylan. I'm sorry. I'm in this condition because I made bad choices and those choices backfired." The tension in Candace's voice eased. "I can't blame anyone else for where I am. I know I need to put my big-girl pants on and deal with where I am."

Kaylan sighed inwardly, and prayed that God would give her the words to say to give Candace some encouragement. She knew Candace was hurting, and she wanted God to use her to be a blessing to her friend. She would wait for God to tell her what to do. "Well, girl-friend, where you're at, it is not permanent," Kaylan said. "You have to first start with God. I know God can help you, and He's willing to take the pieces of your life and put things in order."

Candace nodded her head. "You're right. I know I need to re-dedicate my life to Christ."

Kaylan wasted no time in responding. "We can pray right here if you don't mind."

Candace laughed. "Okay, let's do this." Kaylan extended her hand across the table, and opened her palms as an invitation for Candace to pray with her. Candace eagerly accepted. As they prayed, Kaylan could feel the presence of God. Candace's voice began to shake as she repeated the words.

Minutes later, they finished their prayer and released their hands from one another. When their eyes locked, both were filled with tears. They reached for the tissue on the table and cleaned their faces. Kaylan scooted out her chair and came around the table to give Candace a hug.

"Thank you, Kaylan. This means a lot to me. It feels like a ton of weight was just lifted off my shoulders," Candace said.

"Praise God!" Kaylan said with a smile. "You don't have to thank me; I'm so happy that I was here for you. From this moment forward, we are going to stay connected, all right?"

Candace nodded. "That sounds like a plan. Love you, girlfriend."

"Love you, too, Candace. Well, since we got that cleared up, I can tell you about our girls' weekend that I'm planning," Kaylan said with excitement as she returned to her seat. She couldn't wait to start filling Candace in on the plans. "Well, I've already spoken with Jordan and Tiffany, and they are in. I'm planning on having all of you come to my home in Napa the first weekend in April. Will you be able to come?"

Candace grinned. "Yes. I don't have anything on my calendar. Even if I did, I would make some adjustments. I don't want to miss this. So everyone will be there, huh?"

"Great," Kaylan said. "Yes, everyone will be there. I've contacted one of my friends who owns a day spa, and she's willing to come give us massages. I'm going to have our weekend catered by one of the best companies in Napa County. You won't need to bring anything except some clothes and toiletries. April is a perfect month to do this. The weather is going to be fabulous." Candace sat and looked amazed as Kaylan gave all the details about their weekend retreat.

"Girl, how big is your house, and what about Bryan? You kickin' him out his own house?" They both laughed.

"No," Kaylan chuckled. She reached for her coffee. "We have a two-bedroom, in-law unit in the back of our home that has plenty of room. Since it will be in April, we will set up the massages outside next to the pool."

Candace eyes widened. "You have an in-law unit and a pool, huh? Wow, that's nice. You have pictures of your house?"

"I do." Kaylan reached for her purse that was in the empty chair and took out her iPad. She placed the electronic device in front of her, turned it on, and waited for the menu options to appear. When the camera option came on the screen, she scooted her chair around the table and sat closer to Candace. "Here is my house,"

Kaylan said. She moved the screen from left to right, showing Candace all the pictures of her property from the outside to the inside. Kaylan didn't know how seeing her home made Candace feel, so she waited until Candace gave her the go ahead before showing her the in-law unit.

"Kaylan, this is beautiful, and the decorations are off the chain. So where is the in-law unit?" Candace asked her friend. Kaylan scrolled through her iPad menu and located another file that had all her pictures of the in-law unit.

"Here is the in-law unit." Kaylan once again scrolled the pictures from one direction to another, showing Candace more of the vineyard. Candace peered at the pictures. She could see that Kaylan's life had been blessed. She could only hope that from that day forward, maybe something great would come of her life. After the slide show, Kaylan stood up, grabbed her chair, and placed it back in its previous position, all the while securing her iPad back in her purse.

As the ladies continued their conversation, Kaylan decided to talk about Candace's relationship with

Derrick. Although Candace tried to hold back her tears as she discussed it, Kaylan could feel her pain. "Candace, I'm sorry about Derrick. Do you have any pictures of him?"

"No, we were a very private couple, and never took pictures together. But we were happy. He was trying to help me get myself together, and then the script flipped. But I will always cherish the moments we shared."

Hearing firsthand about Derrick and all that Candace was going through only made Kaylan want to bless her friend the more. Her friend had lost her man and had gotten laid off from her job, but was still standing. A scripture came to Kaylan's mind as she reflected on her friend's situation: "And I will make of you a great nation, and I will bless you [with abundant increase of favors] and make your name famous *and* distinguished, and you will be a blessing [dispensing good to others]." Kaylan leaned back in her chair and said, "Candace, I want to bless you. God has blessed me so I could be a blessing to others."

Candace cocked her head. "Kaylan, you don't have to do any more. I didn't call you to get anything from you other than our reconciliation."

Kaylan sighed. "I know, but this is something I'm led to do. Just receive what I want to do for my girlfriend, okay."

"Okay," Candace retorted. She sat back in her chair and played with her fingers.

Kaylan reached over and grabbed her purse. She pulled out her checkbook and wrote Candace a sizeable check.

When Candace saw that the check was written out for two-thousand dollars, a feeling of guilt and shame came over her. Part of her wanted to tell Kaylan the truth about her former love relationship; yet the other side told her to shut up and take the money. And as she placed the money inside her cross body bad, Candace looked at her friend with a half-smile. Telling her the truth would just have to wait for another day; and she would just have to deal with her guilt later.

Chapter 6

C andace arrived home after her lunch with Kaylan and found it just as she had left it. She walked into her bedroom where she quickly removed her clothes and stepped into the shower. The falling water caused her to relax, enabling her to process what had just transpired.

Her lunch meeting with Kaylan had her re-examining her life, which was filled with so many secrets, secrets that no one else knew, and secrets she'd take to her grave. The guilt would definitely eat her up before she shared with her best friends the double life she had been living.

Her life went on a complete spiral after Derrick died. At least that's the story she had been telling people for quite some time. Truth was, Derrick really wasn't dead. He was very much alive, but his identity prevented Candace from sharing with others their love affair. After numerous disappointments in life, she fell into a deep depression, which led to drinking, smoking, and taking all kinds of prescription pills. When she wanted to finally give up on life, she met this incredible man named Derrick, who helped build her self-esteem again. In essence, Candace felt like this was the love of her life, her hero, the man that God sent to be with her.

But even though she felt this way about him, Derrick was not able to fully commit to her as she wanted. He was married, and although he told her that his marriage was rocky and on the verge of divorce, he was still not ready to end it. This was something that Candace could not accept, so she broke it off with him, only to return to his warm embrace again after being lonely for a week. Derrick seemed to have a hold on her, one that she could not let go.

Drinking, smoking, and sleeping around had no limits, where Candace was concerned. She wanted to stop, but the pull was too hard, and the struggle to quit never did win. She didn't know he was married and had kids, nor did she know to whom he was married. That is until one night when she picked his pocket and found some pictures in his wallet of a beautiful family, a happy family, it seemed. That was the night her dreams ended and the charade began.

As Candace sat in her room, she began to reflect on how they first met. It was a rainy night in December when she decided to grab a bite to eat at Jazzy's restaurant. The holiday season was in full swing. It was a time for people to shop, eat, and enjoy their families. But not for Candace; she hated the holiday season because she had no one to spend that special time with. Trying to get out of an emotional funk, she grabbed her purse, keys, coat, and umbrella and headed out the door, all the while praying that her car would start.

Happy with the sound of the engine running, she hoped her car would get her to the restaurant and back home safely. She put her car in drive, and after thirty minutes, she pulled into the parking lot. She drove around the lot twice before she found an empty parking stall. She unbuckled her seat belt and climbed out of the car. She grabbed her coat from the passenger seat and slid it on. Moments later, she walked into the restaurant.

Just as she figured, Jazzy's was filled with people, laughing and enjoying the casual atmosphere. Instead of waiting for a table, she decided to sit at the bar.

"Why in the world did I do this?" she asked herself. "It is so crowded." She gave the waitress her order, pulled her phone out of her purse, and checked her emails in her Facebook page. Her attention was turned to the groups of people throughout the restaurant who were enjoying each other's company. Her eyes met the eyes of one of the men sitting at the bar. When she saw him looking at her, she immediately re-focused her attention on her phone.

She could feel him staring at her as she tried to concentrate on other things. Each time she looked up, she could see him peering at her. Made uncomfortable by his actions, she glanced at the time on her phone and wondered how long it would be before her meal arrived.

"Excuse me." She looked up at the tall, dark-skinned man who stood before her. It was the man from the opposite end of the bar. "I apologize for interrupting you," he said. "Is the seat next to you taken?" The gentleman stood over her with his hands in the front pockets of his jeans. She took a good whiff of his cologne, which was intoxicating.

She answered slowly, "No. It's not."

"Do you mind if I sit next to you?" he asked cautiously. Before she answered, the waitress arrived with her meal. The waitress placed her chicken salad on the table in front of her and refilled Candace's soda.

"Sure you can," Candace answered as she began to taste her meal selection.

"Would you like to order now, Derrick?" the waitress asked the gentleman sitting next to Candace. Derrick gave the waitress his dinner order. *He must come here a lot; the waitress knows his name,* Candace thought.

"How's your meal?" He paused for her to respond. She took a deep breath before answering.

"It's good," she replied.

"I'm sorry, I haven't properly introduced myself. My name is Derrick." Candace used the linen napkin on her lap to wipe her mouth. She turned and faced Derrick.

"Nice to meet you, Derrick. You must come her quite often; the waitress knows your name." He winked and laughed out loud but didn't answer.

I'm Candace," she chuckled. She thought about how stupid she must have looked and wished she could have changed her response. She felt like a teenager just meeting a boy for the first time. Derrick extended his left hand to meet Candace's. Her eyes lowered to see if a ring was on his finger, but there was none. His grip was firm, yet gentle. She looked at him and wondered why he was being so friendly to her. She didn't come into the restaurant with any intentions of picking up anyone. She had done many things in her life, but picking up men was not one of them. However, after their initial meeting, Candace spent as much time with Derrick as she possibly could. For Candace, meeting Derrick was the best thing to happen to her. No wonder she was in love.

What a complete mess she'd made of her life. How could she look her friends in the face without feeling the guilt?

And how could she attend the retreat and hold her head up high? Those questions raced through her mind, but she didn't have any answers. She knew her past had finally caught up with her and she couldn't hide her sins from the world anymore. She had to accept the consequences of her actions and the possibility of losing the people who mattered most to her, beside Derrick. Candace was emotionally torn in two directions—should she tell the truth about everything and lose everyone, or continue deceiving herself and others?

She emerged from the shower and slid on her oversized tee shirt and sweats. She walked into her kitchen and filled her tea kettle with water. While her water was boiling, she looked through the mail that was on the kitchen table to only find bills. Minutes later, the teapot sounded. She took a cup from the cabinet and poured herself a cup.

Candace took a sip and headed for the living room. She sat on her brown sofa and placed her tea on the table located next to her, before turning on the television. She popped in one of her favorite DVDs from her Tyler Perry collection. Just like those films, Candace felt like her life was filled with a lot of drama. And with all the lies, she began to wonder what part of her life had any truth to it.

Chapter 7

The day that Jordan discovered the text message, she slid on a jogging suit and a white, long-sleeve shirt, and hurried out the house in an effort to escape the pain she had experienced. She called Tiffany to let her know she was on her way over. She got into her car and gripped the steering wheel as tightly as she could. She pulled out of the garage and headed towards Tiffany's house to relieve some stress. Driving down the road, she could only pray that God would give her the strength to face Eric and make the necessary decisions that needed her attention.

Her eyes filled with tears as the honks of other cars managed to interrupt her thoughts of the trauma she was now in. She weaved in and out of the traffic, not knowing what direction her car was taking her. The whispers in her ears kept speaking louder and louder the more she drove. She steered her car until the weeping became so bad that she could not drive anymore. She pulled her car into the nearest lot and parked in the first available stall. Her body was shaking. She prayed that she would make it to Tiffany's house in one piece.

She reached into the glove compartment and found some tissue to clean herself. Who was this woman Eric was seeing behind her back? She couldn't imagine being married all this time and not knowing the double life her husband was living. She felt like a complete fool.

How did we get here? The question echoed through her head. As far as she was concerned, her life was going well. She had a great job and a great husband, so she thought. She had a good church, wonderful friends and two beautiful kids. Now, with a snap of a finger, in a moment's time, her life had changed.

The more she thought about it, the more she wanted to explode. Her cheeks were flushed as the blood inside her began to boil. Thoughts of revenge bombarded her mind. Maybe one of those stories on *Lifetime* could give her an idea of how to get even. She wished she could poison his food or hit him with a bat and get away with it, but she knew she couldn't, because her convictions would not let her. Her brain was telling her one thing and her heart the complete opposite. A vision of the movie, *Waiting to Exhale,* flashed in her mind, especially the scene when Angela Bassett sets her husband's clothes on fire. That seemed like a great way to release some of her anger. She wanted to show Eric just how she really felt. But in her heart of hearts, she knew she couldn't do that either.

"Why can't I get even, Lord?" she yelled. Although she asked this question, within herself she knew the answer.

A still small voice replied, "Vengeance is mine, says the Lord."

"Okay, Lord; but I still want to know who she is." How could she find out who his mistress was? What would she do when, or if, she found out? Would she have the guts to confront her? "I must be totally crazy. I am not in high school anymore. Confronting someone in these times is a sure way to get killed," she said to herself.

Jordan sat engrossed in these thoughts and recounted the events of the day. She believed that it was God who led her to read the text message. She needed to know the truth, no matter how painful the discovery was. Now that she knew that her husband was having an affair, she was determined to find out who this other woman was. Jordan needed help because all she had was a phone number.

She took a deep breath, started up the engine and continued her journey to Tiffany's house. When she finally arrived, she pulled into the driveway and parked her car. She couldn't remember how she got there as safely as she did, because her mind was definitely not on the road. *Had to be my angels*, she thought.

Jordan unfastened her seat belt, grabbed her purse from the passenger seat, and headed towards Tiffany's house. Midway to the door, her cell phone began to ring. She grabbed her phone from out of her purse and saw Eric's face on the screen. Instead of answering his call,

Jordan hit the Ignore button and placed her phone back in her purse.

Jordan rang the doorbell three times before Tiffany answered. When her friend finally opened the door, Jordan looked a complete wreck. Her makeup was smeared, her eyes were bloodshot red, and her hair looked as though she had been in a fight.

"Girl, what is wrong with you? You all right?" Tiffany asked in a high-pitched voice. Jordan rushed into Tiffany's house and plopped herself on the tan, leather sofa in the living room. She threw her purse on the coffee table located in front of the sofa. Tiffany hurried into the kitchen and grabbed Jordan a bottle of water from the refrigerator. Tiffany rushed back into the living room, unscrewed the top, and placed the water on the table.

Jordan didn't think she could possibly have any more tears left, but when Tiffany questioned her again, she let out an uncontrollable cry. Jordan's head collapsed into her hands. Tiffany immediately ran over to her friend and offered her some tissue that was located on the coffee table. Jordan laid her head on Tiffany's shoulder when Tiffany offered a hug to console her.

"What happened?" Tiffany asked again in a gentle tone. Jordan took a sip of the water before she spoke.

"Eric is having an affair." She clutched more tissue and blew her nose. "Can you believe that?" Jordan shook her head. "I just can't believe he would do this to me."

"What do you mean Eric is having an affair?" Tiffany released her grip on Jordan, looking her square in the eyes in disbelief. "What are you talking about, Jordan? Eric adores you," her friend said as she tried to reassure her.

"No!" Jordan yelled. "Eric is sleeping around." She reached for her cell phone, and hit the message button on the screen. Jordan had forwarded the text message that Eric received from the other woman to her phone before she left her house just to show her friend. "Here, see for yourself." She handed Tiffany her cell phone. Tiffany took it and read the message out loud.

"What? You have got to be kidding me," Tiffany said.

"No, and that's not all. Eric asked me for a divorce. He came home today and gave me some lame excuse about getting a divorce. He was talking about how I preached too much to him. And after he left the house, he forgot his phone. That's when I saw that he had a text message, so I read it. Yes, I did. I knew he wasn't telling me the truth. He's a liar and a cheat!" exclaimed Jordan.

Tiffany let her friend vent before responding. "I'm speechless. I just can't believe he would do this to you." Tiffany stared at her friend, and saw the anguish in her eyes. "Who is the woman?" Tiffany, for a moment, forgot her religion, calling his mistress and Eric every foul name in the book.

Tiffany cocked her head to the side. "Girl, what are you going to do about this? Did you confront Eric yet?"

Jordan shook her head. "I haven't confronted him yet, but I am. He doesn't know I read the message." She hesitated. "Well, he might. Eric called me right before I walked in your house." She took a deep breath. "And I have no idea who this woman is, either. All I have is her phone number."

"Give me her phone number," Tiffany insisted. "You want me to call her? I sure will, and tell her a few things."

Jordan shook her head. "Naw. This is something I need to do." Jordan stared at the phone and struggled with the idea of calling the other woman. But she had been through so much. Was she emotionally ready to face the woman who stole her husband's heart? Did she have enough fight in her to have the heart-to-heart talk with his mistress?

After talking more with Tiffany about the situation, Jordan finally decided that she would talk to his mistress to find out what was going on. So she pressed the Talk button, dialed the woman's number, and held her stomach. This was the hardest thing she would ever confront in her life, or so she thought. She had no idea of the storm that was raging her way.

Chapter 8

"I t's finally here. Today is the big day," Kaylan shouted. She arose to a bright and sunny April day. She was so excited that she could barely sleep the night before. She tossed and turned the entire night, only because she wanted this weekend to be perfect. She didn't want anything to go wrong. Today, the sisterhood would be reunited, and today would be the beginning of what she hoped would be more gatherings with her girlfriends.

Weeks of planning and preparation had gone into this retreat. Instead of having her friend come to do the massages, she decided to have the limo pick them up and take them to European Day Spa. The caterer had set up a beautiful display of trays full of fruits, vegetables, and imported cheeses. The bottles of cider were chilled and the meals were fit for a queen. The house was decorated with red roses, carnations, and lilies. The house smelled heavenly. She made a schedule of activities just like a genuine retreat would offer. She knew they would think she'd gone too far with the schedule since it was only the four of them, but Kaylan wanted it to be special. She had purposed to give her girlfriends a treat they'd remember their entire lives.

The weather was perfect. It was projected to be in the 80's the entire weekend. She could not have asked for more. *God is in this,* were her thoughts. Why she hadn't thought to do this earlier, she didn't know. This could turn into an annual event. The more she thought about it, the more thrilled she became.

She hoped and prayed that each one of the ladies would come willing and ready to be healed and made whole. Kaylan was expecting a spiritual breakthrough, not only for herself, but her girlfriends, as well. They were coming together for fun, food, and a spiritual renewal.

Bryan was taking care of Aisha, giving her a weekend full of shopping, movies, and a night of roller skating with five of her friends. Aisha had the entire weekend to get spoiled by her daddy, and she was going to show him exactly how to do it, with her friends included. Aisha had her daddy wrapped around several fingers. He knew it, but didn't mind at all. Aisha was a "daddy's girl".

Kaylan walked into the kitchen and set the table with a white tablecloth, fine China, flatware, crystal goblets, cloth napkins, and tapered, blue candles. For the center-piece, she picked a square, glass vase and filled it with a beautiful bouquet of roses.

She looked at the clock located on the wall; it read 12:00 pm. The limo would be arriving shortly from picking up the ladies. The caterers were doing the last minute touches on the lunch, which consisted of shrimp with linguine, garlic bread, cider, and salad.

The doorbell sounded just as Kaylan was putting the finishing touches on the tablescape. "They are here," she muttered. She trotted to the door and opened it with a breathless sigh. Standing before her were all three of her friends, Tiffany, Jordan, and Candace. The friends stood, giggling; their bright smiles greeted her. But for some reason, Candace's smile didn't seem too genuine. *Something isn't right.* Kaylan felt it in her spirit, but she just didn't know what *it* was.

She fixed her eyes on the limo driver and directed him to put the luggage in the guest house. Kaylan brought her attention back to her friends. *It is going to be an interesting weekend, to say the least,* she thought. "Hello, ladies, welcome to the Vineyards."

"Hi, Kaylan," they said in unison. Tiffany, Jordan, and Candace stood behind each other as Kaylan extended her arms and hugged each one's neck. Kaylan stepped aside to allow room for them to enter. When they walked into the foyer, they placed their purses on the chaise lounge.

Candace's large, brown eyes grew saucer-sized as she surveyed the foyer and the framed African American art that hung on the walls. "Wow. Kaylan, I love those pictures, and this house…it's gorgeous."

Jordan's head went from left to right as she looked from the foyer into the living room. "This is beautiful. I love your house, Kaylan."

"This is breathtaking. Did this house come out of a *Better Homes and Garden* magazine?" Tiffany jokingly asked.

"Thank you," Kaylan said. "Follow me. We will be gathering in the kitchen first and move our way to the guest house after lunch; I will give everyone a guided tour of the house and vineyard. But that's if y'all want one."

"Guest house. Guided tour," Tiffany muttered. They all chuckled. They followed Kaylan into the kitchen. "It smells good in here," Tiffany praised as the aroma of herbs, garlic, and spices filled the air.

The ladies let out a big sigh once they entered the spacious, colonial kitchen. They slowly scanned the kitchen table and admired how beautifully it was decorated. The kitchen had dark, rich-tone cabinetry in a quarter-sawn cherry and pepper-corn finish. The kitchen island and countertops were in pure white. The crystal vase with red roses made a beautiful centerpiece on the kitchen island.

"I'm so happy y'all are here." Kaylan's joy was palpable. "Lunch is ready. Go ahead and take a seat." The ladies pulled out their chairs and sat themselves across from one another. They placed the napkins in their laps and helped themselves to the vegetable, fruit, and cheese trays. After they got their appetizers, the table fell silent. They bowed their heads while Kaylan asked God's blessing over the food and the weekend.

"Kaylan, you did a fantastic job with everything," Jordan said in between bites. One of the caterers came and filled their goblets with chilled, apple-raspberry cider.

"Yes, I agree; it is truly a blessing to be here," Candace said. "Thank you for inviting me."

Tiffany cocked her head to the side. "I can't wait to see what else you and God have in store for us. I've been excited about coming here all week. We have so much to catch up on. So much has happened in our lives."

"Yeah, good and bad," Candace whispered. She turned and faced Kaylan. "Where is your bathroom?"

"Sorry, I guess I should have showed y'all where the bathroom was when you first came in. Does anyone else need to go?" Both Jordan and Tiffany shook their heads. Kaylan jumped up and ushered Candace to the foyer and gave her directions to the bathroom. "Down the hall, first door on your right."

Kaylan reclaimed her seat and told the caterers to bring the hot dish of linguini and the basket of warm, garlic bread to the table. The caterer returned, placing the dishes in the middle of the table and refilled their goblets of cider.

Ten minutes later, Candace reclaimed her seat and leaned back in her chair. She smiled, placed her napkin on her lap, and took a sip of her cider. "That dish looks yummy. Are we supposed to eat all this food?"

"Perfect timing, Candace. I thought you got swallowed up in there," Kaylan said. They all laughed.

"No, I'm good. All is well," she responded. Candace surveyed the kitchen. "Is there dessert, too?"

"Yes. But we can eat dessert outside next to the pool after we relax," Kaylan replied. After they let out a laugh, they resumed eating their lunch. In the meanwhile,

Kaylan handed each one a program on blue linen paper, which listed the entire weekend of events. Reactions of excitement filled the room when they saw that a spa treatment was on the agenda.

"O.M.G.!" Jordan said. "This is wonderful, Kaylan. You sure know how to plan a retreat. I need this more than you know," she said as her voice raised an octave.

Tiffany's eyes glowed. "We all could use this. After the week I've had, this is very timely." She took a swig of cider.

Candace raised her head up from looking over the agenda. "I must admit, this whole experience is totally new for me. In all of my years, I've never had a mud bath, mineral bath, or a body wrap. Shoot, I don't even know what half of that stuff is." All the fuss Kaylan was making for the ladies made Candace feel a little uneasy and guilty. *I wish I could have changed the last years of my life*, she thought.

Kaylan, speaking in a bubbly tone, said, "I'm just happy I can share this experience with all of you."

One hour later, and still completely stuffed, they eased out of the kitchen to begin their activities. Kaylan took the ladies on a tour of the main house, the vineyard, and eventually her parents' home.

The first stop on the tour was the main house and vineyard. It was a magnificent spring mountain villa. Grandeur, serenity, and timeless Mediterranean elegance characterized this palatial estate with panoramic views of Napa Valley. Grand-scale rooms, five fireplaces, a library, an office, wine cellar, and the grounds inspired the kind of serenity found in the world's most secluded villas. While ranking as one of the largest private residences in Napa Valley, it was also an intimate and family-friendly home with a floor plan that maintained privacy for all.

After visiting the vineyard, they were ready for the next item on the agenda: the spa treatment. One hour later and one pound lighter, the ladies were picked up by the limo, which drove them to the spa in Napa County. European Day Spa was the finest and most complete Napa Valley day spa resort in the city. It offered a plethora of luxury spa services, including body scrub, mud bath, mineral bath, and body wrap.

Once they got settled in the limo, they sipped on non-alcoholic beverages, including sprinkling water, cider, and an array of juices. Kaylan wanted to do a toast to the event. So, they lifted up their glasses while Kaylan made a one-minute speech for the occasion.

"While we live separate lives, we are still good friends. Let's make this weekend enjoyable and memorable and unforgettable." With that, each one lightly tapped one another's glass and said, "Cheers."

The limo pulled into the parking lot thirty minutes later. The chauffeur opened the passenger door and helped each one of the ladies get out the car. For the next few hours, they were going to forget about life – at least all the problems – and concentrate totally on relaxing and enjoying the moment.

Right in the heart of Napa County, the view was breathtaking. The engaging landscapes, the Mayacamas Mountains, and small-town charm captured their attention. Together, they walked inside the spa to relish the type of treatment that only a woman could really appreciate.

Once inside, the staff greeted them and led them to a changing area where they were provided a comfortable, woven robe, and then escorted to the mud bath. After fifteen minutes, the attendant guided them to the shower, then into a bubbling, aromatic, mineral tub to relax and further unwind. A blanket wrap followed, swaddling them in all-natural, fresh, cotton blankets. The mud treatment was followed by an excellent, sixty-minute, hot stone massage.

On their ride back to Kaylan's house, they reminisced about the entire day. Each one shared what part of the spa experience they enjoyed the most. Jordan loved the honey body scrub, although the feel of the mud bath was also something to be desired. Candace had to admit that the mud bath was her favorite. Tiffany leaned more toward the hot, stone massage; and Kaylan's favorite was the mud wrap.

When they arrived back at Kaylan's house, she led them to the guest house to slip into something more comfortable, unpack their luggage, and have dessert by the pool. This weekend had started off on a great note.

Chapter 9

A fter a full day at the spa, relaxation by the pool, touring the property, and visiting Kaylan's parents, the ladies refreshed themselves and walked to the main house for dinner. During the planning stages, Kaylan had asked each lady to tell what their favorite meal and favorite dessert were. This weekend was all about them, and she made sure the caterers were well prepared to accommodate their every request.

Tonight's meal consisted of roasted garlic crab, tiger prawns, and noodles. For dessert, the ladies would have Candace's favorite, strawberry cheesecake. The table was superbly set. They pulled out their chairs and made themselves comfortable.

Kaylan and the caterers locked eyes, which was her cue for them to start serving the dishes. They brought to the table a plate for each of the ladies, which consisted of the entire Dungeness crab—roasted to perfection—and large tiger prawns. The garlic noodles were served in a glass casserole dish and placed in the center of the table. The caterers filled their glasses with a non-alcoholic beverage. Once everything was set, they held hands in preparation for a word of prayer. Kaylan asked Tiffany to do the honors.

"Father, in the name of Jesus, thank You for blessing us with this weekend. Thank You for Kaylan, who so graciously opened her home to us. Bless the food and allow it to bring nourishment to our bodies. We rebuke the calories and the fat that this weekend will leave on our hips. In Jesus' name, Amen." After they chuckled, they said, "Amen" in unison.

For the next hour or so, they did not raise their heads, nor did they say a word. They feasted slowly, savoring all the flavors, herbs, and spices from the seafood and noodles. Tonight was not the night to have manners, not with crab and tiger prawns. They licked their lips and fingers and smacked on the food the entire time.

After savoring tonight's meal, the caterers brought them each a warm towel for their hands and mouth. The cheesecake would have to wait until later; they were too stuffed to even consider taking a small slice. But a cup of flavored coffee seemed to hit the spot.

"Jordan, are you okay?" Kaylan peered at her. "Is something bothering you? I can tell you are in another place and time. That's what this weekend is for: so we can bond, get free, and allow God to heal us."

Tiffany moved her chair closer and looked Jordan directly in the eyes. "I'm sure we got a whole lot to talk about this weekend." Tiffany continued to emphasize her point. "These men... I just don't know about them. Some of them don't want to commit, some of them want to sleep around, and some of them don't know when they have a good woman." It appeared that Tiffany wanted to continue her rant, but the look Jordan gave her indicated that it was time to move on. "Oops, my bad. Sorry, Kaylan, you were talking to Jordan, huh?"

The room fell silent. Jordan nodded, but didn't smile. "Something is, but I'll wait 'til later to talk about it. I don't want to spoil our dinner," she said sadly. Kaylan saw the worry in Jordan's eyes as well as her effort to try and control her emotions.

The look of shock was evident on Kaylan's face. Those words pierced her sharply as though a knife had been thrust in her chest. *What in the world was Tiffany talking about when she said "Men sleeping around"? Whose husband was she referring to? Considering there are only two married women at the retreat, she is either talking about Bryan or Eric. And I know she ain't talking about my husband,* Kaylan pondered.

Kaylan took a sip of coffee before she spoke. "Now Tiffany done got me wondering what she's talking about." She stared at Jordan and reached for her hand. "Jordan, when you're ready, we are all ears." Out of the corner of her eye, she took a glimpse at Candace, who was squirming in her seat.

Kaylan leaned back in her chair and looked at the three of them. They had been friends since high school, but she wondered if she really knew them as well as she thought. It was quite obvious that Tiffany knew something about somebody's husband. Jordan was going through a major test, and Candace was uncomfortable, but why? *Lord, please don't let nothing jump off up in here.*

After dinner, they headed over to the guest house to relax, but Jordan could barely contain herself. As much as she tried to suppress her emotions, Jordan doubled over and began sobbing when she entered the living room. Her head collapsed in her hands and her tears were unrestrained. Seeing Kaylan's happy parents only reminded her of the life she wished she could have.

Tiffany and Candace grabbed Jordan, putting their arms around her waist. They ushered her to the white, three-piece sofa and helped her sit down. Tiffany and Candace plopped themselves down, one on each side of her.

Kaylan hurried to the bathroom to get some tissue. When she returned, Jordan reached for one of the tissues and blew her nose. Without being asked and in between the sobs, Jordan told the ladies that Eric had asked for a divorce and was seeing another woman. A disapproving silence filled the air as she continued with her heart-

breaking news. The more she shared, the louder her
voice became.

Kaylan stood directly in front of them and stared at
Jordan intently. She could hear the anguish in her
friend's voice. "What? No, Jordan. Eric is cheating on
you?" She covered her mouth with her hands.

Tiffany rolled her neck and eyes. "Oh, believe it, girl.
Yes, Eric is having an affair with some trifling home
wrecker." Tiffany wasted no time continuing the discus-
sion. "Yeah, and Jordan called the woman, too." But
Jordan didn't want them to know about the phone call.
She did dial the number, but hung up after the phone
connected. She was afraid to face the woman that stole
her husband's heart.

Jordan raised her voice. "Tiffany, is this my story or
what? Let me tell it." Tiffany's eyes grew wide. But she
acknowledged that Jordan was right. It was her story and
her pain, and if she wanted Candace and Kaylan to know
more, it would have to come from her. "I'm so sorry;
please forgive me."

Candace's pulse quickened with guilt. It wasn't easy
to dismiss what she was hearing and seeing. The guilt

was eating her alive. Her stomach was churning. Her palms were sweating. Her heart was pounding so loudly, that she was sure anyone in the room could hear it. She felt like running, but where would she go? How would she get there? She tuned Jordan and the other ladies out and focused on her own plight. She knew if they found out that she was the other woman, they would all give her a beat-down. She might not get out of Napa County alive. *Oh, dear Lord, help me.* No point in calling on the Lord now; this was her mess that she created. *Chalk it up to another bad decision that will probably cost me dearly. There is absolutely nothing good going to come from this. I really hate my life now,* she thought.

Candace first learned about Derrick's wife when she found the photos of his family in his pocket. Since she had lost contact with her friends years ago, she was unaware of who each one had married. When Derrick entered her life, he never made mention of who his wife was, only that they were about to divorce. But when she learned that Jordan was the one, she immediately knew that it had to end. Consequently, Derrick's, or rather Eric's charm was too much for her to relinquish. And because she was no longer close friends with Jordan, she was able to continue the affair without guilt. That is until now.

"Candace, are you listening?" It was obvious that she was engrossed in her own thoughts. "Did you hear Jordan?" Kaylan's voice triggered Candace back to the present.

"I'm sorry. I was just thinking about what Jordan told us," said Candace. *I should come clean before this gets out of hand.* A flashback of Jordan beating up Stacie in high school crossed her mind. *I am so messed up,* Candace thought.

Kaylan spoke. "Jordan said she's going to call the woman right now. She wants to hear what the voice of the home wrecker sounds like. Jordan is ready to face this Goliath and maybe give that woman a good cussing out. Well, Jordan didn't say that last part; that came from me."

Kaylan and Tiffany continued baiting Jordan until she pulled out her cell phone from her purse. She retrieved the number from the sheet of paper she tucked in one of the zippered compartments in her purse, and dialed the number.

When the call went through, it sounded as though the ring was coming from one of the bedrooms. "Whose phone is that ringing?" Kaylan crossed her arms and asked. "It's not mine. My phone is at the main house," Kaylan added.

"My phone is turned off," Tiffany answered.

Jordan pulled the phone away from her ear and stared at Candace. "Where is your phone?" Jordan paused for Candace to respond. But when she didn't, Jordan jumped from the white sofa, dropping the phone on the floor. Jordan and Candace made a mad dash to their bedroom (like two athletes running the 100-yard dash) in search of the ringing phone. When they got in the room, Jordan discovered that the ring was coming from Candace's purse, which was sitting on top of her luggage.

Tiffany and Kaylan looked at each other awkwardly. Tiffany picked the phone up off the floor and disconnected the call. Without hesitation, they followed Candace and Jordan to the bedroom. "If something is going to go down, I am not going to miss any action," Tiffany said under her breath.

"Did you know about this, Tiffany?" Kaylan questioned her.

"No. I'm just as surprised as you are. I know this is not happening. This is wrong on so many levels."

When Tiffany and Kaylan arrived in the room, they witnessed Jordan and Candace having a tug-of-war with Candace's knock-off purse. "Candace, you better not be the other woman. If you are, you ain't getting out of here alive. I'm going to kick your butt something bad," Jordan said angrily.

Tiffany and Kaylan were stunned and speechless. They stood there with their mouths wide open. The last time they heard Jordan talk like that was in high school when she beat the heck out of Stacie Green after the basketball game.

Tiffany and Kaylan jumped in the middle of the brawl. Tiffany grabbed Jordan by the waist while Kaylan grabbed Candace.

"Stop this, right now!" Tiffany yelled.

Kaylan looked intensely at Jordan. "Let the purse go. We are going to find out the truth, right Candace?"

"Okay. If I call that number again and it's your phone, there is going to be some trouble. You know what I mean? Do you get me?" Jordan's eyes glanced at Candace. Tiffany and Kaylan released their grip on the women and stood in front of them.

Sweeping her right hand across her forehead to get rid of sweat, Candace clinched her purse with the other hand.

Kaylan spoke in a quiet voice. "Let's calm down. There is not going to be any fighting going on here. We are adults, and this is going to be handled in an adult manner."

Tiffany chimed in cautiously, "Agreed. Jordan, what happened to those scriptures you been quoting? You can't be fighting nobody. You know what the Bible says: 'For we wrestle not against flesh and blood, but against spirits in high places.' That's how it goes, right?" Tiffany paused and waited for a response.

With her hands on her hips, Jordan said, "You serious?" She let out a long breath. "Tiffany, call the number."

Candace licked her lips and responded, "You don't have to call the number. I'm so sorry, Jordan. I'm the other woman. I have been having an affair with Eric. But it's not what you think. At first I didn't know he was married, and I definitely didn't know he was married to you! I'm so sorry. Please forgive me."

Jordan gasped. Tiffany and Kaylan stared at her with the most disgusted look they could muster. Candace began sobbing uncontrollably, making a spectacle of herself. She begged and pleaded with Jordan for forgiveness.

In between the sobs, Candace began to explain how she and Eric met: "During Christmas, I went out for dinner and there he was at the bar. He approached me and we began talking. Believe me, I didn't go there to pick up any man and I didn't know he was married or married to Jordan. We exchanged phone numbers, and the rest... I don't need to go into all the sordid details."

Jordan wasn't moved by Candace's emotional outburst. One minute later into the theatrics, Jordan shot in between Tiffany and Kaylan, got in Candace's face, and slapped her. Tiffany and Kaylan grabbed Jordan and pulled her away from Candace. Candace looked dazed and stood with her mouth wide open.

Jordan screamed, "How could you, Candace. You know what? Just get out of my face. What you've done is inexcusable."

Confused, Kaylan stared at Candace. "You told me his name was Derrick and that he died." She tilted her head to one side. "What is wrong with you? Who makes up something like that? You're sick!" She raised her voice three octaves.

Tiffany added her two cents. "You should be ashamed of yourself! How dare you smile in our face, all the while knowing that you are sleeping with Jordan's husband! You know what they call women like you? A home wrecker is the polite word."

They waited for her to respond. Her voice cracked. "I don't know what's wrong with me. I am so sorry for hurting all of you." She stared down at the floor. "Please forgive me."

"Shut up!" Jordan ordered. "I don't want to hear another word from those lying lips. Sleeping with my husband? That's low. You know what? Ya'll deserve each other."

Kaylan crossed her arms and jumped in Candace's face. She stood still, but inside she wanted to slap Candace, too. "You come telling me that sorry story about you wanting to change and all the bad decisions you made," Kaylan hollered. "Yada, yada, yada. How could you?"

Tiffany shook her head. They were not buying Candace's confessions or her momentary act of remorse. They were done with her. No matter what she said, or how she said it, they wanted her gone.

"I'm going to call the limo driver to come and pick you up," Kaylan said sadly. "Get your stuff. I just can't believe you would do this. Obviously, your judgment has been clouded."

Chapter 10

Candace picked up her belongings and headed to the front door. Her cries intensified with each step she took. She refused to look back at them because last time she did, their eyes told the story. They loathed her and she knew it; she felt dirty. She grabbed some tissue and waited outside for the limo to arrive. She knew she had lost her friends because of her own self-destructive behavior. Today's disaster had to have been the worst. The guilt and condemnation she felt was even deeper now than ever before.

Ten minutes later, the limo driver pulled up. He walked around and opened the door to the passenger's side, helping Candace get situated. His instructions were to take her back to her apartment. The sound of the limo door closing assured the ladies that she was gone, possibly gone for good, or at least gone for an indefinite period of time.

On the ride back to her place, Candace rehearsed painful memories of past conversations with her mother and sister. Candace's demons of low self-worth, rejection, and insecurities crept in again. The venom in her soul had been there as long as she could remember. She wished she could have stood up against her mother and sister to dismiss their negativity, but courage was not one of her strengths. Those voices were ringing louder and stronger in her mind. "You will never amount to anything. Your life ain't worth living." These words played in her mind like a scratched record. "Maybe they are right. My life is not worth living," she voiced out loud.

Kaylan, Tiffany, and Jordan collected themselves, walked back into the living room, and sat down on the sofa. They continued to console their friend, Jordan, in hopes that something either one of them said would help her deal with what just went down. What was planned as a perfect weekend, had turned into a total catastrophe and an unforgettable experience for all involved. Kaylan knew that Jordan was going to need help dealing with the distrust and betrayal she now felt.

There was a long silence before Kaylan spoke. "Jordan, I am so sorry about what just happened," Kaylan said cautiously. "This definitely is not how I planned this weekend to be."

Tiffany shook her head and eyed Jordan. "I just can't believe what went down."

Tears traveled down Jordan's cheeks. "You can't believe it? Me either. Who would have ever thought my friend would be sleeping with my husband. Her of all people. I am so done with both of them. Y'all should have let me beat her down." Obviously Jordan was distraught. Deep down inside, she knew that was not the answer. Her fighting days were over, but today she put aside all her Biblical teachings.

Kaylan nodded. "I understand how you feel. What are you going to do?"

Jordan twisted her face as if in deep thought. "When I get back home, I'm putting his butt out." A sense of dread came over her. "As much as I believe in marriage and hate divorce, I will not stay with someone who cheated on me. Some lines you just don't cross."

Tiffany raised an eyebrow. "I know that's right. Make sure you call Pastor and talk with him. Counseling right about now will do you some good."

The whole episode made her angrier. Her eyes were protruding and when she spoke, her lips curled. "I just can't believe it. Why would she do this to me?" Jordan questioned. She held back more tears. "I wasn't prepared for this one," she admitted.

"We had lunch a few weeks ago," said Kaylan, "and she told me the dude was dead. I mean, how do people do it? She looked me dead in the face and told me that bold-face lie. I even gave her a fat check to help her get on her feet."

Tiffany leaned forward now. "Oooh wee, Kaylan. I bet you wish you could stop payment on that one. Wow, she fooled you big time." The last thing Kaylan needed at this point was a reminder of how much money she had given Candace. She felt like a complete fool. The one person she thought wouldn't take advantage of her generosity tricked her out of a bundle.

Jordan's eyes widened. "She had absolutely no conviction then and definitely no conviction now. That show she put on today did not move me one bit. The nerve of her."

"Hold that thought." Kaylan stood and strolled to the kitchen to get something cold to drink for the women. She grabbed the bottles of water from the refrigerator and retuned a minute later. She handed them the water bottles. They unscrewed the caps and took a swig.

After reclaiming her seat, she leaned back on the couch. Kaylan offered a slight smile. "Even though Candace has hurt us, there is a lesson I believe God is trying to teach us. No one is more hurt than Jordan; that goes without saying. Deception is no friend to anyone. Regardless of what she did, we have been Christians long enough to know that we have to practice what our pastors have been preaching to us."

"Well, I'm just going to be honest. I am too overwhelmed with all these emotions to even think right."

Jordan's emotions were pulling her in many different directions. She was furious, battered, and heartbroken. The pieces of her life had crumbled right before her eyes. Yet, there was a peace she felt, but could not understand.

Tiffany looked stone-faced. "I know. Sometimes forgiving is so hard, especially when you have been hurt really bad." She took a sip of her water. "Sometimes the person you love the most could be the person you should distrust the most."

Jordan arched forward and peered at Kaylan. "Although I'm totally ticked off, hurt, disappointed, and want to lash out, I know the Word of God will help us get through these trials. I know we must forgive because if we don't, God will not forgive us."

"As long as I've been saved, I never experienced anything like this," Tiffany confessed.

Jordan chimed in. "Last week's sermon was taken from Deuteronomy 20:4 'For the Lord your God is He who goes with you, to fight for you against your enemies, to save you.' Well ladies, I flunked this test, big time. I realized I got all in the flesh." Her lower lip quivered while explaining her behavior. "I slapped

Candace. That was so wrong. Just like I have to forgive Candace and Eric, I need God to forgive me."

Tiffany and Kaylan nodded. They knew she was telling the truth. She was not the only person that had crossed the line today. Although Candace's behavior was erroneous and unthinkable, they too allowed their flesh to rise. They had all heard sermons that would have at least prepared them for how to handle the situation in a more tactful manner.

Jordan reached for more tissue from the table. She was wounded and scared from the traumatic experience. She hurt so much, but couldn't fully articulate how deeply her pain went to the women. The thought of Eric touching Candace, let alone having sex with her, turned Jordan's stomach. She could only pray that God would walk with her, guide her, and bring something good out of this situation. But at the moment, all hope of anything good coming from this seemed gone; her only trust had to be in God.

"Jordan, if you need to stay here, you can for as long as you like. This is a great place for solitude and to seek the Lord," Kaylan offered.

Kaylan's offer humbled Jordan. "Oh, thank you. That's so nice of you to offer. I just might take you up on that." Jordan didn't know what to do at first. She was grateful that she had a job and wasn't like a lot of other women who didn't work, depending solely on their husbands for everything. That was one thing about Jordan: she knew how to bounce back, but she'd be the first to admit, this had turned her world upside down.

Tiffany hesitated before replying. "We still have two more days here, unless what has happened has cancelled the rest of our retreat. I mean, we could pray now and believe God that He'll begin the process of healing. There's no time like the present."

"Most definitely," answered Kaylan. "No. We could continue as planned, unless Jordan is ready to go back home. It's up to her." Jordan didn't know what kind of company she'd be, but she wasn't ready to go back home.

"No, let's use the remaining time here as planned, minus one. God knew this was going to happen," replied Jordan. "I want to use this time to do what a retreat is supposed to do: refresh, rejuvenate, and restore. And what I really need is to get in God's face."

Today, the living room was going to be their sanctuary, that place where they hoped to find answers and lay all their burdens down. This was going to be their individual time with God. They all had their own trials, needs, struggles, and tests. With the chain of events that happened today, a divine encounter with God was not just needed, but desired.

Kaylan stood up and walked to the stereo where she popped in a worship CD, and listened to the songs from Israel Houghton, CeCe Winans, and Donnie McClurkin. The atmosphere was set for worship. The melodies to the songs seemed to make all their problems, worries, and anxieties go away. Then they lowered their knees and prostrated themselves for prayer.

Kaylan began the worship with prayers unto God: "Lord, You see where we are; we are hurting. Help us deal with what has happened this weekend. We pray that Candace comes to the knowledge of the truth, that she repents of her actions, and gets saved." When words were not enough, they worshipped. The more they worshipped, the more the presence of God filled the room, and the Holy Spirit began to remind them of certain scriptures pertaining to their requests.

Tiffany petitioned the Lord concerning their families, their jobs, and direction for their lives. "Lord, Your Word says that all things will work together for good. We pray that no matter what happens in life, Your will shall be done."

When it came time for Jordan to pray, all she could muster up was her tears. In between the sobs, she was asking the Lord to guide her steps. "Father, hear my cry. Help me forgive Candace and Eric. Show me my purpose." In between their time, they worshipped and lifted up their hands as a sign of surrender.

After an hour of communing with God, they stood up and reclaimed their seats on the couch. They sat quietly, waiting to hear more from God and to receive the answers to their requests.

Once they concluded their prayers, they decided to turn in for the evening. Tomorrow was going to be another full day, but they were determined not to let what happened ruin the rest of the weekend.

Chapter 11

Six months later....

On Saturday morning, Jordan crawled out of her king-size bed and headed towards the bathroom to take a soothing bath. She lined the tub with vanilla-scented candles. She slowly undressed, then eased herself into the tub. For twenty minutes, she tried to enjoy the aromatherapy and allow the bath to relax her weary body, but visions of the past still caused her heart to ache.

She spent the last six months trying to get adjusted to being single again. *You can spend your entire life wanting to be in a long-lasting relationship, and just when you think you've found the person, the rug is snatched right from under you,* she thought. The person that said 'change hurts' wasn't lying. She knew that all too well.

She had filed for divorce from Eric and was slowly getting her life in order... very slowly. Eric had moved out and moved on, which meant rearranging her house to her specifications, sleeping alone, and eating by herself. Those three things were a continuous reminder that her fairytale had ended. She thought she'd married the man of her dreams—her college sweetheart and soul mate. She decided it was time for her to move on, too.

She didn't realize how difficult the transition was going to be. At times, she questioned her own ability to stand. *Can I do this? Am I strong enough?* She'd buckle at the knees with the weight of everything she was facing, but God was her rock.

"Being alone sucks," she said to herself. Many days she fought depression and loneliness. Some days were better than others. It was still hard for her to accept how her life had changed. But she was determined to press through the days and long nights and not let what she was experiencing defeat her. She was taking it a day at a time. Her pastor told her that 'better days would come'. She would cling to that word forever.

One thing she could attest to, and that was her walk with Christ was growing stronger. Her prayer life had gone up to another level and her study time had increased. She was learning how to hear from God more clearly.

Nonetheless, she knew one decision, one deceptive act, one wrong turn in life made all the difference in the world. The consequences of Eric's and Candace's behavior left a bitter taste in her mouth. No ifs, ands, or buts about it; she was still heartbroken.

She stepped out of the bathroom and slipped into some leggings and a tee shirt. Minutes later, she walked into her kitchen where she prepared herself a cup of hazelnut coffee. She sat down at the kitchen table with her Bible, notebook, and tablet when suddenly she heard the Lord say to her spirit, "All is not lost."

<><><>

Kaylan woke up from her nap to what she thought was a nightmare. She lay in bed with the covers over her body, staring at the ceiling, trying to make sense of what she felt in her spirit. She'd tossed and turned the night before, but this time she was feeling uneasy because she knew something was not right. She whispered, "Lord what's wrong with Candace? Something is very wrong."

Since the retreat, she had been in prayer for all of them, Candace, Jordan, and Tiffany. She knew Jordan was still heartbroken and torn; and Tiffany, at times, could hold a grudge, but she'd come around sooner or later. She prayed earnestly for their relationship, but most importantly, for Candace's salvation. Candace needed to have a genuine encounter with the Lord. No religion or religious experience, but she needed to be "born again". (The old folks used to say "born anew").

Candace's actions showed that she had some internal demons and strongholds that followed her throughout the years. Their friend was a "hot mess" and no one would dispute that. But Kaylan knew that God specialized in helping those who were a "hot mess".

"Lord, I don't know what to do. You know her plight, her situation, and what is going on now with her. What can I do?" Kaylan reached for her cell phone on the nightstand to check the time; it was 5:30 p.m. She rolled out of her king-size bed and placed her feet in her slippers. She marched down the hall to her office to do some work and to call Candace.

Once inside, she walked to her desk and pulled out her brown, leather chair. She turned on her *Surface* tablet, checked her emails, surfed the Internet, and purchased a new Dooney and Bourke bag off of QVC.

It had been six months since the incident that occurred with Candace. No one, including Kaylan, had reached out to connect with Candace. After all, what did anyone have to say to her? And why would they? She was the one who offended, backstabbed, and hurt them.

Kaylan had been saved long enough to know that God would require the more mature Christian to make amends. That's where she came in. Apparently, God wanted either the relationships to be reconciled or He wanted Candace truly saved, or both. Either way, Candace was now her project.

If it was up to Kaylan, she wouldn't try to reach out, because it felt like she'd be disloyal to Jordan. But it wasn't about being disloyal; it was about obeying God and doing what Kaylan believed was right, not according to any one person, but right according to God. Even if they never spent any more time with Candace, they still needed to forgive her, as hard as it was.

She did have one thing holding her back, though. Kaylan wasn't sure what to say to her or how to approach her. All she knew was that God had placed Candace on her heart. Jordan and Tiffany would not understand her trying to reconnect with someone who did what Candace had done.

For the next sixty minutes, Kaylan looked over her work schedule for the upcoming week. She tried to gather her thoughts and face the inevitable — calling Candace. She leaned back in her chair and took a deep breath before dialing the number. She stared at her cell phone with hesitation. Nonetheless, she hit the Contacts button on her phone and searched in her list; but as soon as she punched in her number, a call came in from Tiffany.

"Hey, Tiffany, what's up?" she answered.

"Gurrrl, have you heard about Candace?" Tiffany sounded flabbergasted. Kaylan leaned forward and listened eagerly. Tiffany's tone was a true indication that something dreadful had happened to Candace. She had Kaylan's full attention. *Are my questions going to be answered in the next few seconds?* she wondered.

"I just got off the phone with a reliable source who told me that Candace tried to commit suicide."

Kaylan was so surprised; her mouth fell open. "What?" Kaylan's voice raised an octave. "Where is she? How is she doing?"

"Slow your roll, Kaylan. One question at a time. She is at John Muir Hospital in Walnut Creek."

"When did this happen?" Kaylan grilled.

There was a long silence before Tiffany spoke again. "She was brought in last night." Kaylan detected the uneasiness in her voice. "They pumped her stomach. She's still alive."

"I wonder who is with her. I know her family is not there. I wonder if they know," Kaylan asked, genuinely concerned. "I'm sure she's all alone."

"Oh, well," Tiffany retorted.

"Tiffany, don't be so heartless. She's still our friend who just happens to be messed up. She needs us. She needs Jesus, too," Kaylan said with concern.

"Speak for yourself. I mean, she doesn't need us," Tiffany shot back.

"How would you feel if we didn't come to your aid, or come see you if something like this happened to you?" Kaylan asked.

"Well, first of all, I don't sleep with married men, especially my friends' husbands. That's just foul. Secondly, the Bible says that whatever a man sows, that shall he reap."

"Wow. Tiffany, we have to show compassion; we give mercy to receive mercy. The Bible says He does not retain His anger forever, because He delights in *mercy*. When a person tries to commit suicide, it's because of some deeper, internal problems. It's a spiritual battle that goes on in the soul of the person. I know… because I wanted to commit suicide before," Kaylan explained.

"What?" Tiffany shouted. "You never told me. Why would someone of your caliber, status, and wealth want to end her life?"

"Well, I have to tell you that story some other time, but for now, it's about Candace. This confirms my dream."

"What dream?" Tiffany questioned.

"The Lord woke me up this morning to pray for Candace. I knew it was something terrible, but I didn't know it was this. In fact, I was about to call her right before you called."

Tiffany was shocked. "Really?"

"Candace needs to see a psychiatrist or psychologist. Maybe now she will get the help she needs. Don't get me wrong; I believe Jesus can touch her and make her whole, but she first needs to believe and want His help," Kaylan explained. "Yes, when Jesus truly is Lord over our lives, He makes all the difference."

Tiffany agreed. "Amen."

"We need to see her," Kaylan stressed. "That's the least we can do. Can't you lay aside how you feel about her for a moment? We have to forgive, and this is one way we can show it."

Tiffany knew Kaylan was serious about seeing Candace, but Tiffany didn't know how Jordan was going to react to the news of the hospital visit. After all, Jordan's feelings mattered, too. Kaylan paused, waiting for her to respond.

"You're right, and she does need to be ministered to. I know I need to forgive her, as well. If y'all can forgive her, I know I can, too," said Tiffany.

"Have you told Jordan the news?" Kaylan questioned.

"Yes. I called her before calling you. But which one of us will be the one to tell her we are going to visit Candace? She did ask if we were going to visit her, so, she kinda figured we might."

"It doesn't matter. I don't think Jordan is going to be mad at either one of us. Why don't we do a three-way call?"

"That's a great idea. Let me get her on the line."

When the call connected, Jordan answered on the first ring. They explained to her that they wanted to go and visit Candace. Without hesitation, Jordan concurred, and surprisingly, she wanted to join them. Jordan was still hurt, but she decided to show mercy and grace and to walk in forgiveness. They didn't know what the future was going to hold for their relationship with Candace, but they were reminded of one scripture: "Work at getting along with each other and with God...Make sure no one gets left out of God's generosity" (Hebrews 12:14 The Message). Together, with God's help, they would do everything in their power to mend what had been broken.

About the Author

Beginning her career in 2008, Paulette is an award-winning, bestselling, award-winning author and the founder of **WNL Coaching and Marketing Services**. She is the author of several books and founder of **Write Now Literary Virtual Book Tours,** a service to help promote authors of the Christian genre and authors of clean books.

As an inspirational and motivational speaker, Paulette's desire is to empower, influence and cultivate women to move forward while dealing with issues that hinder women from becoming all they are created to be. Her topics are biblically sound and pertinent to the needs of today's women. Paulette is a wife, mother, grandmother and Bible teacher. Paulette has appeared on numerous radio and Television shows.

Combining enthusiasm with an energetic speaking style, audiences describe Paulette's presentation as inspiring, enriching and encouraging. She is committed to speaking a message that is always uplifting and edifying.

As a writing coach, she is the visionary behind her own writing ministry called "**Write Now,**" a literary program that specializes in coaching aspiring writers in the areas of creativity, development, and publication of Christian books. She provides her listeners with tools, resources, and opportunities to help them succeed in the writing business.

*Also available
by
Paulette Harper*

Also available
by
Paulette Harper

Also available
by
Paulette Harper

THE SANCTUARY

PAULETTE HARPER-JOHNSON

*Also available
by
Paulette Harper*

THAT WAS THEN, THIS IS NOW
this broken vessel restored

PAULETTE HARPER

www.ingramcontent.com/pod-product-compliance
Lightning Source LLC
Chambersburg PA
CBHW071308130626
46556CB00004B/1516